Each squirrel had a little sack and
a large oar and spread out his tail for
a sail.

They also took with them an
offering of three fat mice as a present
for Old Brown and put them down upon
his doorstep.

Then Twinkleberry and the other
little squirrels each made a low bow and
said politely, "Old Mr. Brown, will you
grant us permission to gather nuts upon
your island?"

But Nutkin was excessively rude in
his manners. He bobbed up and down
like a little red cherry, singing,

"Riddle me, riddle me, rot-tot-tote!

A little wee man, in a red red coat!

A staff in his hand and a stone in his throat;

If you'll tell me this riddle,

I'll give you a goat."

Now this riddle is as old as the hills. Mr. Brown paid no attention whatever to Nutkin.

He shut his eyes stubbornly and went
to sleep.

The squirrels filled their little sacks with
nuts and sailed away home in the evening.

But next morning, they all came back
again to Owl Island. And Twinkleberry
and the others brought a fine fat mole and
laid it on the stone in front of Old Brown's
doorway, and said,

"Mr. Brown, will you grant us
your gracious permission to gather some
more nuts?"

But Nutkin, who had no respect, began
to dance up and down, tickling old Mr.
Brown with a nettle and singing,

"Old Mr. B! Riddle-me-ree!

Hitty Pitty within the wall,

Hitty Pitty without the wall;

If you touch Hitty Pitty,

Hitty Pitty will bite you!"

Mr. Brown woke up suddenly and carried the mole into his house.

He shut the door in Nutkin's face. Presently, a little thread of blue smoke

from a wood fire came up from the top of
the tree, and Nutkin peeped through the
keyhole and sang,

> *"A house full, a hole full!*
> *And you cannot gather a bowl full!"*

The squirrels searched for nuts all over
the island and filled their little sacks.

But Nutkin gathered oak apples—
yellow and scarlet—and sat upon a beech
stump playing marbles and watching the
door of old Mr. Brown.

On the third day, the squirrels got
up very early and went fishing. They
caught seven fat minnows as a present for
Old Brown.

They paddled over the lake and
landed under a crooked chestnut tree on
Owl Island.

Twinkleberry and six other little
squirrels each carried a fat minnow, but
Nutkin, who had no nice manners,

brought no present at all. He ran in
front, singing,

> *"The man in the wilderness said to me,*
> *'How many strawberries grow in the sea?'*
> *I answered him as I thought good—*
> *'As many red herrings as grow in the wood.' "*

But old Mr. Brown took no interest
in riddles—not even when the answer
was provided for him.

On the fourth day, the squirrels
brought a present of six fat beetles, which
were as good as plums in plum pudding
for Old Brown. Each beetle was wrapped
up carefully in a leaf, fastened with a
pine-needle pin.

But Nutkin sang as rudely as ever,

"Old Mr. B! Riddle-me-ree,

Flour of England, fruit of Spain,

Met together in a shower of rain.

Put in a bag tied round with a string,

If you'll tell me this riddle,

I'll give you a ring!"

Which was ridiculous of Nutkin, because he had not got any ring to give to Old Brown.

The other squirrels hunted up and down the nut bushes, but Nutkin gathered robin's pincushions off a briar bush and stuck them full of pine-needle pins.

On the fifth day, the squirrels brought
a present of wild honey. It was so sweet and
sticky that they licked their fingers as they
put it down upon the stone. They had stolen
it out of a bumble bee's nest on the tippitty
top of the hill.

But Nutkin skipped up and down, singing,

"Hum-a-bum, buzz, buzz!

Hum-a-bum, buzz!

As I went over Tipple-tine

I met a flock of bonny swine;

Some yellow nacked, some yellow backed!

They were the very bonniest swine

That e'er went over Tipple-tine."

Old Mr. Brown turned up his eyes in disgust at the rudeness of Nutkin.

But he ate up the honey!

The squirrels filled their little sacks with nuts.

But Nutkin sat upon a big flat rock and bowled with a crab apple and green fir cones.

On the sixth day, which was Saturday, the squirrels came again for the last time. They brought a new-laid egg in a little rush basket as a last parting present for Old Brown.

But Nutkin ran in front laughing and shouting,

"Humpty Dumpty lies in the beck,
With a white counterpane round his neck,
Forty doctors and forty wrights,
Cannot put Humpty Dumpty to rights!"

Now old Mr. Brown took an interest in eggs. He opened one eye and shut it again. But still he did not speak.

Nutkin became more and more impertinent,

"Old Mr. B! Old Mr. B!

Hickamore, Hackamore,

on the King's kitchen door.

All the King's horses and all the King's men,

Couldn't drive Hickamore, Hackamore,

Off the King's kitchen door."

Nutkin danced up and down like a sunbeam, but still Old Brown said nothing at all.

Nutkin began again,

"Arthur O'Bower has broken his band,

He comes roaring up the land!

The King of Scots with all his power,

Cannot turn Arthur of the Bower!"

Nutkin made a whirring noise to sound like the wind, and he took a running jump right onto the head of Old Brown!

Then all at once, there was a commotion and a struggle and a loud "squeak!"

The other squirrels scuttered away
into the bushes.

When they came back very cautiously,
peeping around the tree, there was
Old Brown sitting on his doorstep, quite
still, with his eyes closed, as if nothing
had happened.

But Nutkin was in his vest pocket!

This looks like the end of the story,
but it isn't.

Old Brown carried Nutkin into
his house and held him up by the tail,
intending to skin him. But Nutkin
pulled so very hard that his tail broke

in two, and he dashed up the staircase
and escaped out of the attic window.

And to this day, if you meet Nutkin
up a tree and ask him a riddle, he will
throw sticks at you and stamp his feet and
scold and shout,

"*Cuck-cuck-cuck-cur-r-r-cuck-k-k!*"

About Beatrix Potter

When Beatrix Potter (1866–1943) was growing up in England, she did not go to a regular school. Instead, she stayed at home and was educated by a governess. Beatrix didn't have many playmates, other than her brother, but she had numerous pets, including birds, mice, lizards, and snakes. She enjoyed drawing her pets, and they later served as inspiration for her books.

As a young girl, Beatrix enjoyed going for walks in the country. She began drawing the animals and plants she saw. For several years, she also kept a secret journal, written in her own special code. The journal's code was not understood until after Beatrix died.

In 1893, when Potter was twenty-seven years old, she wrote a story for a little boy who was sick. That story became *The Tale of Peter Rabbit*. In 1902, the book was published and featured illustrations drawn by Potter herself. Her next book was *The Tale of Squirrel Nutkin*, which was published in 1903. Potter went on to write twenty-three books, all that were easy for children to read.

When Potter was in her forties, she bought a place called Hill Top Farm in England. She began breeding sheep and

became a respected farmer. She was concerned about the farmland and preserving natural places. When she died, Potter left all of her property, about 4,000 acres (1,600 hectares), to England's National Trust. This land is now part of the Lake District National Park. Today, the National Trust manages the Beatrix Potter Gallery, which displays her original book illustrations.

ABOUT WENDY RASMUSSEN

Drawing from the time she could hold her first crayon, Wendy Rasmussen grew up on a farm in southern New Jersey surrounded by the animals and things that often appear in her work. Rasmussen studied both biology and art in college. Today she illustrates children's books, as well as medical and natural-science books.

Today, Rasmussen lives in Bucks County, Pennsylvania, with her black Labrador Caley and her cat Josephine. When not in her studio, Rasmussen can usually be found somewhere in the garden or kayaking on the Delaware River.

OTHER WORKS BY BEATRIX POTTER

The Tale of Peter Rabbit (1902)

The Tale of Squirrel Nutkin (1903)

The Tailor of Gloucester (1903)

The Tale of Benjamin Bunny (1904)

The Tale of Two Bad Mice (1904)

The Tale of Mrs. Tiggy-Winkle (1905)

The Tale of the Pie and the Patty-Pan (1905)

The Tale of Mr. Jeremy Fisher (1906)

The Story of a Fierce Bad Rabbit (1906)

The Story of Miss Moppet (1906)

The Tale of Tom Kitten (1907)

The Tale of Jemima Puddle-Duck (1908)

The Tale of Samuel Whiskers or, The Roly-Poly Pudding (1908)

The Tale of the Flopsy Bunnies (1909)

The Tale of Ginger and Pickles (1909)

The Tale of Mrs. Tittlemouse (1910)

The Tale of Timmy Tiptoes (1911)

The Tale of Mr. Tod (1912)

The Tale of Pigling Bland (1913)

Appley Dapply's Nursery Rhymes (1917)

The Tale of Johnny Town-Mouse (1918)